D0475119

Glossary and Pronunciation Guide

Mandarin, the official national language of China, uses a logographic, or picture-based, writing system. The following words have been transliterated into the English alphabet and are accompanied by their English pronunciations.

Bàba 爸爸 (BAH-bah) Daddy

Huashan park 华山儿童公园 (HWAH-shan) Park and playground in Shanghai

hùkǒu 户口 (HOO-koh) A complex system of household registration used in mainland China that works like a domestic passport. A hùkǒu record identifies a person as a rural or urban dweller, based on what hùkǒu her mother has, and can limit her ability to move, hold a job, purchase food, or access government services.

Lìlíng 莉玲 (LEE-leeng) A common Chinese girl's name. Translated from the Mandarin, it means "sound of white jasmine."

lychee 荔枝 (LEE-chee) Also known as a Chinese cherry. A sweet, juicy fruit that grows in bunches. To eat a lychee, peel the reddish-pink skin, then pop the white fruit into your mouth.

Māma 妈妈 (MAH-mah) Mommy

nǐ hǎo 你好 (NEE how) Hello

Qíqi 琪琪 (CHEE-chee) A Chinese girl's name. Translated from the Mandarin, it means "fine jade."

renminbi 人民币 (REN-min-bee) Official Chinese currency

Tǔbāozi 土包子 (too-BOW-zi) An insulting term sometimes used by children. Literally, it means "little dirt bun" and is similar to the American slur "country bumpkin"—someone from the country who doesn't know anything about the city.

Yéye 爷爷 (YEH yeh) Paternal grandfather

To Dad,
who taught me
to live with integrity
and compassion

Special thanks to Chris
and Gloria Hsieh, Libby
Chen, and Sarah Wu,
who helped make sure
all the details of this
book are accurate

 Published in the United States by Anne Schwartz Books, an imprint of Random House Children's Books, a division of Penguin Random House LLC, New York. Anne Schwartz Books and the colophon are trademarks of Penguin Random House LLC.
Visit us on the Web! rhcbooks.com
Educators and librarians, for a variety of teaching tools, visit us at RHTeachersLibrarians.com
Library of Congress Cataloging-in-Publication Data is available upon request.
ISBN 978-0-593-18192-8 (hardcover) | ISBN 978-0-593-18193-5 (lib. bdg.) | ISBN 978-0-593-18194-2 (ebook)
The text of this book is set in 13-point Amasis.
The illustrations were rendered in pencil and watercolor on watercolor paper.
Book design by Sarah Hokanson
MANUFACTURED IN SINGAPORE 10 9 8 7 6 5 4 3 2 1 First Edition
Random House Children's Books supports the First Amendment
and celebrates the right to read.

ALONE
LIKE ME

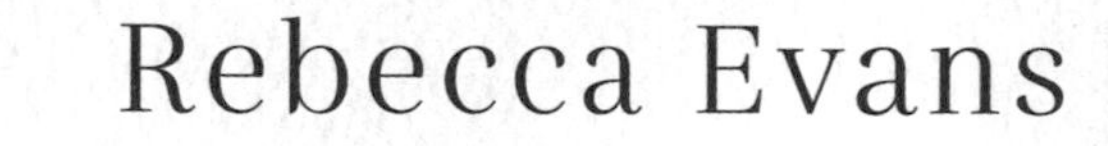
Rebecca Evans

a·s·b
anne schwartz books

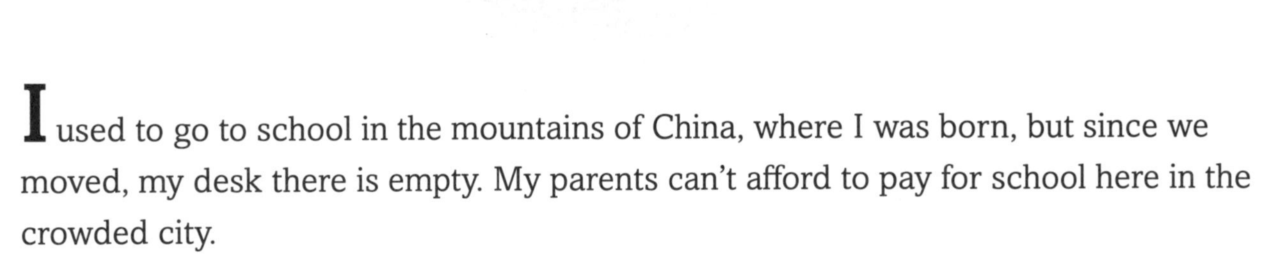

I used to go to school in the mountains of China, where I was born, but since we moved, my desk there is empty. My parents can't afford to pay for school here in the crowded city.

Most days I go to work with Māma, but little girls don't belong in the sewing factory. "Be quiet. No wiggling," they say.

Sometimes Bàba takes me to work. But the can factory isn't a place for little girls, either. "No running," they say.

One day I go shopping with Māma. She holds my hand tight because little girls don't belong at the busy market. There are so many people. Baskets bursting with hot peppers. Pools of fish, turtles, scorpions, and frogs. Piles of steaming dumplings. Puppies bark-bark-barking at bright birds in cages . . .

and a girl in a yellow coat, who smiles at me.

Māma pulls me away before I can smile back. “Hurry, Lìlíng,” she says. “We have lots to do.”

I look for the smiling girl everywhere—behind the spices that make my eyes water,

by the barrels of sweet lychees . . .

under the tables of rainbow fabric.

She's gone.

That evening, Bàba takes me to Huashan park when he gets home from work. "Little girls always belong at the park," he says.

"Nǐ hǎo." I smile at the children, but they laugh at my old red coat and dirty shoes.

"Tǔbāozi!" they call me. Little dirt bun.

I climb under the slide and pretend I'm a dragon with diamond scales. Dragons don't need new friends.

Back at our tiny apartment, I stand on the balcony and watch the big busy city. Down between the tall buildings, thousands of teeny-tiny cars and bicycles zip around and around, on the streets, all full of people, people, and more people.

Something flashes below—sunshine yellow.

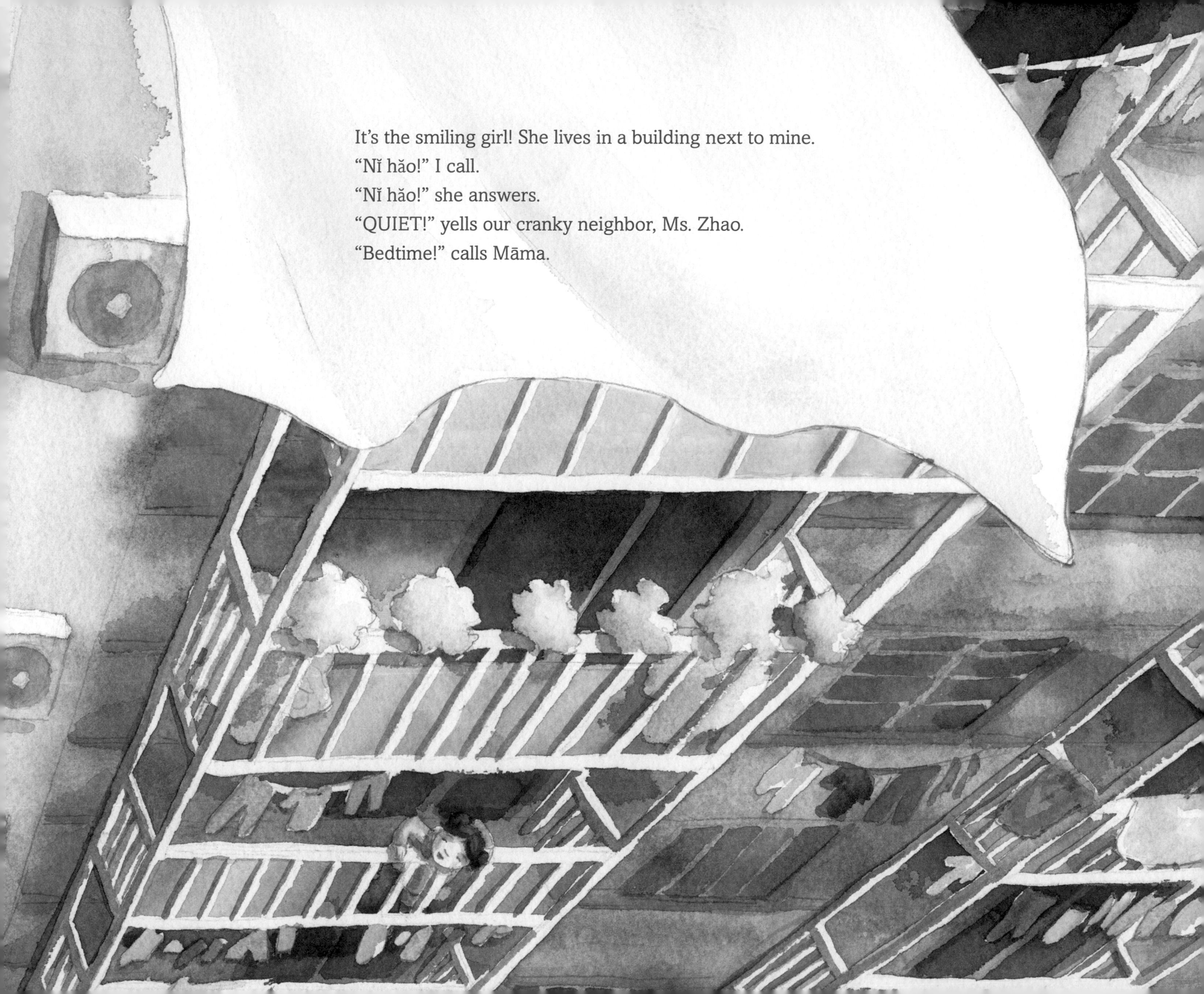

It’s the smiling girl! She lives in a building next to mine.
“Nǐ hǎo!” I call.
“Nǐ hǎo!” she answers.
“QUIET!” yells our cranky neighbor, Ms. Zhao.
“Bedtime!” calls Māma.

The next day, I wait forever while the sewing machines clickety-clickety-click. Finally, it's time to go home.

I run to our balcony. The girl is on her balcony, too. She smiles up at me.

"What's your name?" I shout.

"NO YELLING!" hollers Ms. Zhao.

Now, every night, just before bed, the girl and I smile at each other from our balconies.

I look for the girl when Māma takes me to the market, but she's not there.

I beg Bàba to take me to the park. The girl is not there, either. The kids throw sand at me. “Go back to your farm, Tŭbāozi.”

I climb back into my hiding hole under the slide and pretend it's my secret dragon cave. Even dragons need a place to cry sometimes.

I'm quiet as Bàba and I walk home.

Quiet as we eat dinner. Quiet as I climb into bed. If the smiling girl had been at the park, would she have played with me?

And then I have a big idea!

The next morning, I draw a picture of my old home and friends in the mountains. I write, **Nǐ hǎo, I am Lìlíng.**

你好,我是莉玲。

I stick my note in a can and tie a string around the outside. That night, I lower it over the balcony into the girl's hands.

The next day, I write a new note. **Your yellow coat is pretty. It makes you look like a little yellow ricebird. From your friend Lilíng.**

I lower the can again, and when I pull it back up, there's a new paper inside with a drawing.

I am Qíqi. I used to live on a mountain, too. It was covered in giant snowflakes, it says.

Qíqi and I start writing every day. In the morning, she goes with her yéye to help clean sidewalks. Qíqi thinks it's funny that I call her a yellow bird. She calls me a red ginger flower.

One day, Qíqi writes a special letter that makes me happy.

Dear best friend,

Tomorrow Yéye can take us both to the park. Can you come?

Little Bird Qíqi

I run to ask Bàba so I can write back right away!

Dear Little Bird Qíqi,

Bàba says I can come! But what if the other kids are mean?

Red Flower

Dear Red Flower,
We can be fierce tigers and CHOMP their mean words.
Little Bird Qíqi

Dear Little Bird Qíqi,

We can be mighty dragons roaring over the clouds. Not afraid of anything!

Red Dragon Flower

Today, I take a deep breath and squeeze Qíqi's hand tight at the entrance to Huashan park.

"Remember, we are dragons!" Qíqi whispers.

"Or tigers," I growl.

And we are brave, together.

Author's Note

In 2014, when first I visited Hangzhou and Guangzhou, China, I was captivated by what I saw and experienced—temples built thousands of years before my country even existed, teeming outdoor markets, bicycles that greatly outnumbered cars, and people who actively sought to speak with us. I especially loved the hidden alleyways alive with activity and filled with the rhythm of bike wheels against the pavement. One day, back at home, I painted a picture of an image that had stuck with me from our trip—a little girl perched on a bicycle seat, riding among a sea of other bicycles. I could remember her sad face vividly, because we had not seen many children during the day in the cities. I wondered why. I began to ask questions and do research, to try to understand China better. That's when I heard about the hùkǒu system.

In China, when a child is born, the government gives her papers called hùkǒu, which she keeps for her whole life. The papers state that the only place she can legally have access to free public school, get a job with benefits, or buy a house is in the town where her papers were issued. Because public services in the cities are superior, those with urban hùkǒu papers attend better schools and receive better health care than those holding rural hùkǒu papers. When someone moves, it is possible to get new hùkǒu papers, but it is hard; there are many rules, and each city has different laws.

As China's economy grows stronger, the wealth gap between rural and urban Chinese is narrowing, and more people from the country are able to afford to move to the city. The hùkǒu system is changing as well; it is less restrictive than it was in the past. However, there are still many people who don't meet the requirements or don't have the money to get a new hùkǒu, making it difficult for families to relocate. If children come to the city without new hùkǒu papers—like Lìlíng in this fictional story—they must pay expensive fees to attend public school and may be discriminated against because they are considered second-class citizens. Because of this, most parents who move to the city are unable to bring their children with them. They make the hard choice to leave their children behind in the country with grandparents or neighbors.

When I learned about how difficult the hùkǒu system can make life for poor families, I wanted to share this with others. I know I have much to learn, but I believe the more people strive to understand and respect one another, the more we can work together to make the world a better place.

I also wanted to share a universal story about loneliness and hope. Everyone feels lonely sometimes, but you never know when a new friend might walk into your life and change it forever.

Resources

- abc.net.au/news/2016-09-06/millions-of-chinas-children-left-behind/7816010
- china-briefing.com/news/china-hukou-system-shanghai-benefits-eligibility-application-process
- cnn.com/2014/02/04/world/asia/china-children-left-behind/index.html
- pbs.org/newshour/show/millions-of-chinese-children-fend-for-themselves-when-parents-must-follow-work-far-away
- studio-anrikevisser.com/child-friendly-factory-spaces-in-china
- thoughtco.com/chinas-hukou-system-1434424